Take A Good Look

This story shows that even tiny things
are important and that we must all
take good care of the world.

Story by:
Ken Forsse

Illustrated by:
David High
Russell Hicks
Valerie Edwards
Rennie Rau

WORLDS OF WONDER™

Grubby™ Newton Gimmick™ Princess Aruzia™ Leota™ Wooly What's-It™ Fobs™

Prince Arin™

We're back...and we've got lots of food.

Gimmick showed us what he was so excited about.

Gimmick's machine really did work! We were tiny! It was amazing!

We waited for a long time but Fuzz wouldn't leave.

We crawled out onto the top of the couch.

Look at the size of
that pencil!

Look how big that
strawberry is!

Hey! Look at this
mushroom!

Here's a pretzel!

We saw a spool of thread.

We looked at the pollen on a flower.

We looked at a leaf.

Those are normal grains of salt!

There's some sugar!

We made our way back
to the white circle and the
remote device.

Take a good look at
the world.